Wild Blue

In memory of Rebekah
DS

For Luca
LH

Text copyright © 2023 by Dashka Slater
Illustrations copyright © 2023 by Laura Hughes

First edition 2023

Library of Congress Catalog Card Number pending
ISBN 978-1-5362-1567-0

22 23 24 25 26 27 CCP 10 9 8 7 6 5 4 3 2 1

Printed in Shenzhen, Guangdong, China

This book was typeset in Cheltenham Book.
The illustrations were done in acrylic ink.

Candlewick Press
99 Dover Street
Somerville, Massachusetts 02144

www.candlewick.com

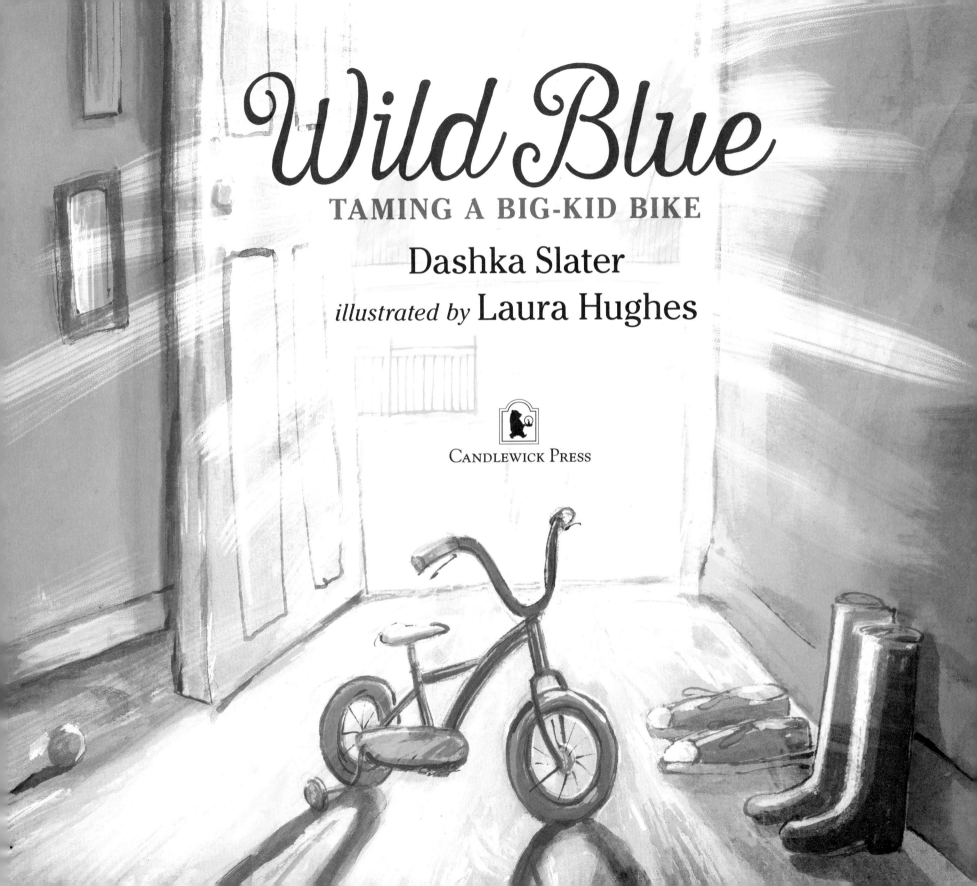

Wild Blue

TAMING A BIG-KID BIKE

Dashka Slater

illustrated by Laura Hughes

CANDLEWICK PRESS

My pink pony and I ride the wide open spaces from sunrise to sunset until my daddy says, "You've grown, Kayla. You're too big for that itty-bitty bike."

Then he puts my pony out to pasture

and takes me to wrangle a new one from the herd.

I name her Wild Blue.

Daddy helps me saddle her up.

Then I take the reins.

"We're going places," I tell her.

But Wild Blue bucks me off.

"Daddy!" I yell. "This bike's not tame enough to ride!"

"You have to get right back on," Daddy says.

"Show her who's boss."

So I do. But Wild Blue bucks me off.

Again.

And again.

"She's too spirited," I say. "I want my pink pony back."

But Daddy just wheels his red stallion from the stable
and puts my brother in the back saddle.

"Let's go to the park," he says.

"You can practice there."

At the park, I check her spokes for breaks

and her frame for scrapes.

I sing her a little riding song:

"Gentle bike, good bike, nice bike,
you don't have to buck and kick.
You can roll slowy-slow,
yippety-yi-yi-yippety-yo."

Daddy asks, "Are you planning
to ride that bike today?"
"Maybe," I say.

Taming a wild blue bicycle takes time.

I comb Wild Blue's mane and stroke her flanks.
We watch the other bikes whiz by,
cantering and galloping.

Wild Blue lifts her head. Sniffs the wind.

She trills her bell, a wild bike whinny.

She wants to run and so do I.

"Go ahead," Daddy says.

I put one foot over and rest it on the stirrup.

I look around to see if anybody's watching.
Wild Blue gets nervous when people stare.

I push off with my other foot.

Wild Blue goes slow and a little wobbly,
because she's not sure who's in charge.
I'm not sure who's in charge, either,
but I know it's supposed to be me.
So I pedal hard until we stop wobbling.

And then we ride.

Around the playground

down to the tennis courts

up to the snack bar

and across the wild blue prairie.

Her legs are my legs.

Her mane, my mane.

Her breath, my breath.

"Looks like you tamed that bicycle," Daddy says.

I shake my head. Nope.

"She's still wild," I say.

"But so am I."